Lobster Fishing on the Sea

Text by Maureen Hull
Illustrations by Brenda Jones

For Jasper
love the
Nana
xx
oooo

Lobster Fishing on the Sea

Text by Maureen Hull
Illustrations by Brenda Jones

NIMBUS
PUBLISHING

Nimbus Publishing Limited
PO Box 9166, Halifax, NS B3K 5M8
(902) 455-4286 nimbus.ca

Printed and bound in Canada

Library and Archives Canada Cataloguing In Publication

Hull, Maureen, 1949-
Lobster fishing on the sea / Maureen Hull ; Brenda Jones, illustrator.
ISBN 978-1-55109-754-1

I. Jones, Brenda, 1953- II. Title.
PS8565.U542L63 2010   jC813'.54   C2009-907270-X

We acknowledge the financial support of the Government of Canada through the Book Publishing Industry Development Program (BPIDP) and the Canada Council, and of the Province of Nova Scotia through the Department of Tourism, Culture and Heritage for our publishing activities.

An earlier version of Lobster Fishing on the Sea, titled Lobster Fishing on the Susan B, was created as an ebook for the River John Library, Pictou Co. Written by Maureen Hull, illustrated by Brenda Jones, animated by David Carlson and Fern MacDonald, and narrated by Joan MacKeigan, it can be seen at www.parl.ns.ca/ebooks/ebooks.htm.

For Marley, Sophie, and Josephine

One Saturday morning, Susan went lobster fishing. It was still dark when her dad woke her up.

"Breakfast time," he said. "We have to get up early to catch lobsters."

"Maybe we'll catch a blue lobster," said Susan.

"Maybe," said her dad.

Most lobsters are dark green and orange, but they can be other colours, too. They can be black, brown, white, red, or blue.

Susan and her dad ate a good breakfast.

Then Susan put on warm clothes, because mornings are cold out on the ocean, even in June. She also put on rubber boots. It's very wet on a lobster boat, and Susan did not want to get cold, wet feet.

Susan and her dad drove to the wharf.

Dad started the boat engine and Susan untied the lines from the wharf. Dad coiled the bow line at the front of the boat. He coiled the stern line at the back of the boat.

Susan climbed down the ladder and got on board. She put on her life jacket.

"Safety first," said Dad.

They sailed out to the fishing grounds. There were many, many buoys floating on the sea.

"Each fisher paints his buoys different colours," said Dad. "The red-and-yellow ones are ours."

Susan hooked a red-and-yellow buoy with a gaff.

"Good catch," said her dad.

A gaff is a long pole with a hook on the end. Susan used it to rescue a bucket she dropped overboard.

"Why are there so many seagulls out here?" said Susan.

"They're hoping you'll drop some bait overboard," said her dad, "instead of an empty bucket."

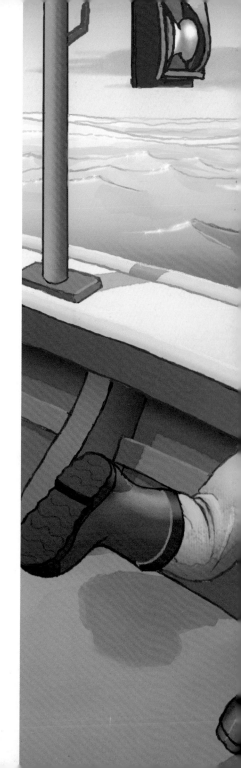

Susan's dad pulled the first trawl into the boat. A trawl is made of traps tied to a long rope. The traps sit on the sea bottom with bait inside to catch lobsters. A buoy is tied to each end of the rope and the buoys float on top of the water.

There were seven lobsters in the first trawl. Susan and her dad put them in the lobster tank.

When all the traps were empty, Susan and her dad put bait bags full of raw herring in each one. Then Dad pushed the traps back into the water, one by one, as Susan slowly steered the boat in a straight line.

Then they picked up another trawl. In it, Susan found four lobsters and two rock crabs.

"There are hundreds of different kinds of crabs," said her dad. "The pea crab is as small as a pea. The Japanese spider crab is as big as a rowboat!"

"These are just ordinary crabs," said Susan. "They aren't really made of rocks."

"No," said her dad, "but they like to hide in the rocks on the sea bottom."

Susan put the rock crabs in the crab tank.

In the third trawl, Susan found more lobsters, more rock crabs, and three purple starfish. "We should make a sign," said Susan. "NO STARFISH ALLOWED!"

"Starfish can't read," said Dad. "They have eyespots at the end of each arm that can only see dark and light."

Susan put her fingers over the eyespots.

"Peek-a-boo!" she said. She put the starfish back in the sea.

In the fourth trawl, she found a sculpin. The little fish had a big head, covered with sharp spines.

"If he were bigger, he'd be very scary," said Susan.

"Be careful," said Dad. "He might be small, but those spines can sting you, like a bee."

Susan put the sculpin back in the sea—very carefully. She didn't get stung.

In the fifth trawl, two hermit crabs were hiding under a bait bag. Hermit crabs live in empty shells they find on the sea bottom. The hermit crabs were very shy.

They made their claws into shell doors, and hid behind them.

"They have beautiful blue eyes," said Susan as she put the hermit crabs back in the sea.

Susan found more and more lobsters, and more and more other creatures.

There were rock eels and a lumpfish.

The rock eels were so wiggly that they tied themselves in knots. Then they wiggled themselves out of the knots. Susan put the rock eels back in the sea. They were so wiggly that she had to use two hands to pick them up.

The lumpfish was bright pink!

"Watch," said Dad. He stuck the lumpfish onto the cabin door, and it stayed there!

"How did you do that?" asked Susan.

"Lumpfish have suckers on their bellies so they can stick themselves to rocks on the sea bottom," said Dad.

Susan wanted to take the lumpfish home because he was so pretty. But she didn't.

"I don't think he likes it there," said Susan. She put the lumpfish back in the sea.

After a long morning of work, it was finally time for lunch.

Dad turned off the engine, and Susan got out the lunch box. They sat on the engine box in the sunshine. They had peanut butter sandwiches and chocolate chip cookies and blueberry juice.

"This is much better than raw herring," said Susan.

"Not to a lobster," said Dad.

Finally all the trawls had been hauled, baited, and put back in the sea.

Susan and her dad sailed back to the wharf with their fish tanks full of lobsters and crabs. They sold their catch to a fish buyer. Fish buyers sell lobsters and crabs to restaurants and grocery stores.

Dad kept one bucket of lobsters to take home.

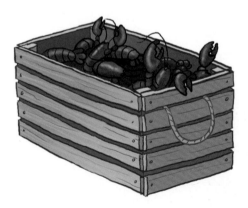

That evening, Susan and her dad had lobster chowder for supper. It was delicious!

"But we didn't catch a blue lobster," said Susan.

"No, we caught a pink lumpfish instead," said Dad. "Maybe next time."

"Yes," said Susan. "You never know what you might find at the bottom of the sea."